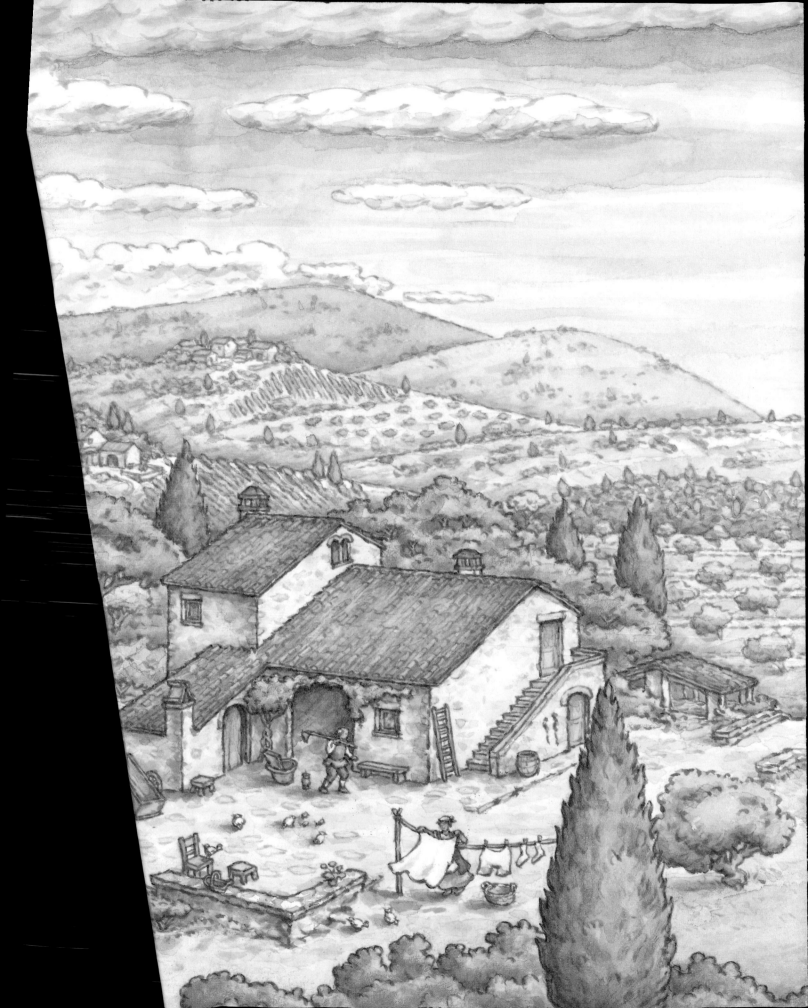

Caterina
The Clever Farm Girl

a tale from Italy retold by **Julienne Peterson**

pictures by **Enzo Giannini**

Dial Books for Young Readers ✦ *New York*

mortar with pestle   *pestle*

A mortar is a strong bowllike vessel. A pestle, which is club-shaped, is hand-held and
used to crush the contents of the mortar to make a powder or paste.
The mortar and pestle are often made of stone and have been used since ancient times
in preparing food and medicine.

Published by Dial Books for Young Readers / A Division of Penguin Books USA Inc.
375 Hudson Street / New York, New York 10014

Text copyright © 1996 by Julienne Peterson
Pictures copyright © 1996 by Enzo Giannini
All rights reserved / Designed by Amelia Lau Carling
Printed in Hong Kong
First Edition
1 3 5 7 9 10 8 6 4 2

Library of Congress Cataloging in Publication Data
Peterson, Julienne. Caterina, the clever farm girl: a tale from Italy /
retold by Julienne Peterson; pictures by Enzo Giannini. —1st ed.   p. cm.
Summary: In this Tuscan folktale, a poor farmer's daughter becomes queen
by charming the king with her wit and ingenuity.
ISBN 0-8037-1181-6 (trade).—ISBN 0-8037-1182-4 (library)
[1. Fairy tales. 2. Folklore—Italy.] I. Giannini, Enzo, ill. II. Title.
PZ8.P443Cat 1996   398.2—dc20   [E]   93-15161   CIP   AC

The full-color artwork was prepared using ink, watercolor, and colored pencils.
It was then scanner-separated and reproduced in red, blue, yellow, and black halftones.

To Sylvia and John, with love
J.P. and E.G.

Caterina, the Clever Farm Girl *is based on several versions
of an old Tuscan folktale known by an assortment of names, including
"The Mortar of Gold," "Griselda," and "The Clever Farmgirl."
These versions were collected and retold by
Gherardo Nerucci (1828–1906), and appeared in his
book of local folklore entitled* Sessanta Novelle Popolare Montalesi
*(Firenze, Successori Le Monnier, 1880).
The architecture and landscapes reflect Tuscany.
For instance, the Savonarola chair (behind Caterina on page 16
where she and the king are standing and talking) is a typically
Florentine chair of the fifteenth century, which is still used today in libraries
and studies, and for weary tourists in the Bargello Museum. The lion crest
(on the fireplace on page 26) is the emblem of the Davanzati family, dating from
the 1200's, whose palace is now the Museum of the Florentine House.
The artist, who lives part-time in Florence, has drawn
the statues and furniture from memory of his beloved native country and
with the aim of conveying an overall Tuscan feel. They are not, however, meant
as exact replicas and may include some variations by the artist.*

Once upon a time there was a poor farmer who lived tending his vineyard. One day he found an object buried deep under some vines. And when he had cleaned off the dirt, he saw that it was a mortar made of gold.

The farmer hurried home to show the treasure to his daughter. "I will give this golden mortar to the king," stated the farmer. "Maybe he will give me a fine reward."

"Don't be silly, Father," answered his daughter, who was called Caterina. "The king will not be satisfied with your gift, and he will say:

'What good is a mortar of gold
Without a gold pestle to hold?'"

The farmer decided not to listen to Caterina's advice, and the next day he took the golden mortar to the king.

The farmer couldn't believe his ears when the king said:

"What good is a mortar of gold
Without a gold pestle to hold?"

"But that's just what my daughter told me you'd say, Your Majesty!" cried the farmer.

"A most remarkable girl," reflected the king. "I think I should see just how remarkable. Take this pound of raw linen and tell your daughter to spin it and weave it into a cloth the length of one hundred arms, by tomorrow."

That evening the farmer did not want to tell Caterina of his encounter with the king, but he felt he had no choice. And he showed her the pound of raw linen.

Caterina shook the linen and three small wooden slivers, which are often found in raw linen, fell to the ground.

"Here, Father," she said, picking them up, "take these to the king and tell him I'll be happy to do the spinning and weaving if he will build a loom for me out of these three slivers."

The next day the farmer returned to the palace, and this time he followed his daughter's advice. The king seemed more impressed than ever with the girl's cleverness.

"I'd like to meet this daughter of yours," stated the king. "Have her come to the palace, neither hungry nor full, neither dressed nor undressed, not on foot, not on horseback, not by day, not by night."

The farmer returned home and nearly cried as he told his daughter of the king's order.

"Don't worry, Father, just find me a fishnet," she said.

Before dawn the next day Caterina rose and ate only an egg. She dressed in the fishnet, with her hair half-combed, half-not. She sat on a goat with one foot on its back and the other on the ground, and at that dawn hour between night and day Caterina arrived at the palace.

"What a wonder you are, Caterina," said the king after a witty conversation in the royal throne room. "Will you marry me?"

"I will if my father consents, Your Majesty," answered Caterina. But Caterina's father had some doubts.

"Be careful, my child, for he is a willful man and he is king. I will keep your room here ever ready should you wish to return home."

So Caterina and the king were married, and everyone celebrated at the gala wedding feast.

Now, one of the king's important duties was to settle disputes for his subjects. The new queen sat beside her husband and often disagreed with his decisions. This annoyed the king, and he forbade her to appear in court again.

One day the king was asked to judge a disagreement between two farmers.

"Your Majesty," began Farmer Antonio, "I came to town to sell my cow at the fair. The stables were full so I asked this farmer if I could tie her to his cart for the night.

"This morning I returned to find she had given birth to a calf, but Farmer Bruno claims the calf is his!"

"That's right, Your Majesty!" cried Farmer Bruno. "It was my cart, so it's my calf!"

The king scratched his head and said, "Right! The calf belongs to the farmer with the cart and we'll hear no more!"

Farmer Antonio, the owner of the cow, could not understand such injustice, and neither could anyone else in the courtroom. "It wasn't like this," they said, "when Queen Caterina sat at his side."

Farmer Antonio decided to find the queen and ask for her help. He went to the royal housekeeper but was told the queen wasn't there. As he was leaving, he passed by the royal gardens and peeked in. He saw a lady. She didn't have a crown on her head, nor was she a great beauty, but there was something about her that made the farmer think that she must be the queen.

Farmer Antonio slipped through the hedges, and told her his tale.

"Ah, that husband of mine," sighed the queen. "There's not much I can do, for he has forbidden me to interfere....But if you will not reveal me, I will give you this advice:

"Tomorrow the king will go out hunting in the Great Woods. In the heart of the woods is a lake, dry as a bone at this time of year. You must dress as a fisherman and pretend you are fishing with a net in your hands. The king will stop and laugh and ask why you are fishing in a lake without water. And you must answer, 'Majesty, there's a better chance of catching a fish here on dry land than a cart giving birth to a calf.'"

And so it was.

The king at such an answer shouted, "This smells of the queen's counsel!" and he stared hard at the farmer.

But Farmer Antonio held his silence.

"Very well," the king said at last, "I was wrong and the calf is rightly yours and shall be returned to you."

The farmer was about to thank the king, but the king was already galloping toward the palace.

"Caterina!" shouted the king as he entered the royal hall. Caterina came down the grand stair.

"Caterina!" he screamed. "You have disobeyed me! You must return to your father's house. Take from the palace that which is most dear to you, and go. This palace is not big enough for both of us."

"As you wish, my dear," said Caterina softly. "But I ask a favor. May I stay for a last supper with you tonight?"

The king agreed and Caterina went directly to the royal kitchens. She ordered the royal cook to prepare roasts of lamb, pork, and wild boar, the king's favorite ravioli, anchovy toasts, roasted nuts, and salty sage biscuits. "And to quench the king's thirst tonight," she instructed the royal wine steward, "I want the oldest and strongest wines from our cellar."

The supper was magnificent, and salty, as the queen had ordered. And after consuming much food and wine, the king fell sound asleep in his royal dining chair.

"Pick him up, chair and all, and follow me," whispered the queen to the servants.

And off they all went to the house of Caterina's father.

"Deposit him here," said Caterina, pointing to her old bed, "and return to the palace." Then Caterina fell asleep beside her husband.

"What rough sheets these are," mumbled the king, half-asleep the next morning. "And what a hard bed." Then he heard the baa-ing of sheep, and he opened his eyes to a low-beamed, very un-royal ceiling.

"Where are we?" he asked his wife.

"Didn't Your Majesty tell me that I must return to my father's house? And didn't you tell me to take with me that which I hold most dear? And so I have."

Then the king laughed and hugged his queen. And from that day the king kept his wife by his side, especially in court, and there was justice and happiness in the land.

As for the golden mortar, the queen still keeps it on her dresser for her royal hairpins; and her father is probably in his vineyard this very minute, still digging around for a pestle.

This story ends well all told,
For wisdom is richer than gold.